Edward "Ned" Hector

Revolutionary War Hero - Time Traveler

by
Noah Lewis & Loretta Graham

• PROJECT FUNDED BY •
Just for the Kids
Education   Foundation

First published by AuthorHouse 10/10/05

ISBN: 1-4208-6817-9 (sc)

Printed in the United States of America
Bloomington, Indiana

This book is printed on acid-free paper.

authorHOUSE

1663 LIBERTY DRIVE
BLOOMINGTON, INDIANA 47403
(800) 839-8640
www.authorhouse.com

History was just another dead subject
until Mrs. Jessup's fifth grade met

Ned Hector.

**Revolutionary War Hero -
Time Traveler**

The day started like all the rest--nothing seemed out of the ordinary. The sun rays revealed speckles of dust dancing in the light, playing tag in the air.

Eric Morris was about to aim a spitball at Megan McDonald, who was reciting the Declaration of Independence. Megan had a cold and her voice sounded stuffy. She kept wiping her nose as she read. Some children were snoring, slumped in their seats. Others were watching the minute hand on the clock, mouthing silent prayers for a fire drill. Laura Wilson was creating an elaborate doodle onto her notebook. Most of the class would agree that history class was a good place for daydreaming.

Suddenly!

Out of nowhere, a man ran shouting into the classroom. All the children jumped to attention. Diane Thompson screamed. The rest of the children stifled giggles and looked to their teacher, Mrs. Jessup, for an explanation for this strange interruption.

The man was dressed in some sort of uniform and on his head was a black hat. Dazed and confused, he ran over to the window. With a look of panic, he shouted, "Everybody down! The Red Coats have broken through the lines!" Then he asked, "Where are they?" He looked around with astonishment. He directed the next question to the startled class:

"Who are YOU?"

Mrs. Jessup was just as stunned as the children, but managed to ask the stranger, "Who are you?" The man reached into his vest pocket and pulled out a piece of folded paper. "Madam, these are my orders." He spoke with an odd accent--sort of British, sort of American. He handed Mrs. Jessup the paper, which she read aloud:

March 10, 1777

Let it be known that Edward "Ned" Hector has been assigned to Captain Hercules Courtney's unit of the 3rd Pennsylvania Artillery Company, from which he is ordered to report to Colonel Proctor's Regiment in Brandywine, Pennsylvania for the defense of Philadelphia. There under the command of General Washington he is to serve to halt and repel the advancing British forces.

Signed,
Continental Congress
George Washington
Commander in Chief of the Continental Army

The soldier stood silently as his orders were read. The children sat dumbfounded and intrigued that their history class had been turned into a real, live history event. "I am Edward Hector," he declared, "but my friends call me Ned. What bewitchery is this? Pray tell me lad, just where am I?"

He was just as confused as the schoolchildren. Jonathan Hunter called out the name of the school, Delaware County Elementary, near Philadelphia. Now Ned was truly bewildered.

"Near Philadelphia?" he asked himself slowly. "With all respect, the last thing I remember is the Redcoats coming up behind our cannon position on the battlefield. The boys were surprised and unable to turn the cannons around fast enough. Once the Colonel gave the order to retreat, everybody ran. The battle was hot and hard and many lost their lives."

The children leaned in to listen as Ned continued his story. Never had they paid attention like this!

"I wanted to run like everyone else," Ned continued, "but my team of horses and the wagon filled with powder and bullets had to be driven out of the way of the advancing Redcoats. I made up my mind not to let the Redcoats capture my horses and wagon. I remember seeing the Redcoats charging across the field."

Ned's eyes were filled with drama and excitement, and so were the children's. "I jumped onto the wagon. I mumbled a quick prayer and urged the horses to a full gallop.

In doing so, I led them out of the line of fire and kept our supplies out of their thieving hands. I ran into an odd fog and I came out here." Ned looked around, still bewildered.

Something up in the corner of the room caught his eye. "I don't mean to be discourteous, but what are these strange things?" He asked, poking his gun at an overhanging TV set. "How is it you get light out of the ceiling without fire?" He was all the more curious and confused.

"Where are all the horses? Why do you build your carriages in such a strange fashion? And why are you all dressed so oddly?" The children looked at each other. "It is you that is dressed funny!" Ashley-Faith said with indignation, "not us, Mr. Hector."

5

"The date! What is the date lass?" Ned demanded from Emily.

"It's Tuesday," she replies matter of factly.

"NO! The year?" he asked with the same sense of urgency.

"2000" Emily said, hardly believing he didn't know. Ned staggered back. The shock was evident on his face.

"Are you all right, Ned?" a concerned Matt asked.

Ned's face brightened, and then he laughed triumphantly, as if he had just figured out a well kept secret. "So you seek to jest with me? You seek to make a fool of me, do you? Very well then I will play along with your jest. However, if it be true that this is indeed the year 2000 as you claim, then that would mean you are from my future." The kids nodded very enthusiastically. "And if that be true," he continued "Then you will have knowledge of my history." With an 'I got you' intoned in his voice he declared. "Then pray, tell me why did we rebel? One child raised her hand, "because of the taxes." Another, said "we wanted to rule ourselves." Someone in the back responded, "The king was being unfair!" Mrs. Jessup beamed with pride. Ned, astonished, replied "Aye, you do know."

Ned seemed to resolve whatever doubt he had in his head. "In truth it would explain your odd appearance and the strange objects here." "Was it really like that, Ned?" Sarah inquired. "Most assuredly, my good girl," Ned replied. "Imagine, there is a knock upon the door, and when you answer it there stands a redcoat staring at you. He informs you that he will be staying at your home. He goes on to inform you that you will feed him, tend to his needs, and give him a place to sleep! With a glance toward his fellow lobster backs, he asks you if you will be causing any trouble. You know there is but one right answer. Ned, kneeling eye to eye with Sarah, asks, "Do you think that fair? Would you want to be treated in such a fashion? How would you feel if you were treated in such a manner?"

Sarah shook her head in disdain and replied, "I would really hate it!" Andrew blurted out, "I would be mad if someone did that to my family." "Absolutely!" Ned reacted. "Or if you would, imagine that a representative of His Majesty comes to you demanding a payment, 'Pay up! Your taxes are due.' And with that he lays out his hand. Now these are taxes that you had no say in. There was not anyone representing you in the British government, no one pleading your case as to whether you could bear this tax, a burden or not. And yet you must pay it."

Unexpectedly, in furious tones Ned shouts, "HOW DARE ENGLAND TREAT US AS IF WE ARE SLAVES! We are British! We have the rights of Englishmen!" The class recoiled in surprise. Taking a moment to compose himself, Ned turned to the startled listeners. "My apologies, dear friends, I meant no offense. But how would you feel if your rights were taken from you?" It was obvious Ned had struck a sympathetic note. "I know how I feel when I'm treated unfairly," offered Mary. "Justly so and well said!" quipped Ned with a smile, making an effort to change the mood.

"How things have changed," he said with wonder. "How things have changed." Seeming a bit more relaxed, he went on. "When I was young, Negro boys and girls rarely were allowed to attend school. Our parents did what they could to educate us, but they had to be very careful, because it was against the law in some states to teach colored folks." Ned looked around the classroom. "Even little white girls usually did not attend school. A girl was expected to stay home and learn to take care of the children and the house.

There was a murmur that rose throughout the room, which was decidedly female in tone. One girl turning to talk to the girl behind her said, "I'm glad I'm not stupid like they were." But as they both giggled, they noticed that the room became very quiet. Upon turning around Julie was startled to find Ned standing in front of her desk. His face showed obvious annoyance. "So you think our women are stupid, do you? By the age of seventeen our young women can control the operations of an entire household single handedly. The head woman in the house is trained well enough to take care of most medical needs of the family and workers living there. If I came to you with an ache in my belly, how would you help me?" "Tums!" she responded with a smile. "They can't run down to the corner store and buy medicine.

They have to make their own," chimed in Mrs. Jessup. "You go out to your garden and pick chamomile and mint to brew for them," Ned continued. "Can you take the flax plant, strip off the fibers spin those fibers into thread, then weave that thread into cloth and make clothing out of that cloth?" Julie, red faced, not knowing quite what to say, shook her head. Ned bent eye to eye with Julie, "Do you understand lass? Just because the women of my time do not have the book learning you are privy to does not mean they are stupid. There are many ways to learn." Ned gave her a "no offense taken" type of smile and continued.

I am amazed to see you all learning together. I am grateful that my parents wanted me to read, write, and know numbers. I want you to know I own a business back where I come from."

All the children asked Ned in unison, "WHAT DO YOU DO?

WHERE DO YOU COME FROM?"

Ned grinned and put his hand to his mouth as if to hide his amusement. "I am a Teamster," he said proudly, "which means I am a Wagoneer or Wagon Driver. I work for myself to support my family. Folks in the city ask me to supply and deliver materials such as fabrics, food, and lumber, anything that folks need to live.

Lately, I've been handling gunpowder for the Continental Army, even though this job is most dangerous. It is my job to bring supplies and important ammunitions. I deliver goods like rifles, gunpowder and cannons to support General Washington and the American Soldiers in our fight for independence against the British Redcoats. My horses make my job easy. I truly wish you all could see my horses.

The entire class was grinning ear to ear. Everybody could picture a team of handsome horses standing; ready to gallop into action at the sound of Ned's voice. Ned continued. "As your teacher just read to you, I was given an official order to work with the Continental Army.

There is not a team of horses as fast or as fine as mine on this side of the Delaware. Of this, I am very proud. I surely do love my horses."

Michael Collins raised his hand. "How could a black man fight in the Revolutionary War," he asked, "if all blacks were slaves?"

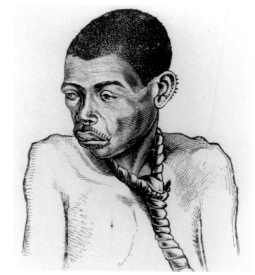

Ned answered the question by repeating that he was a free man operating his own business. "I am saving my money. My wife and I are hoping to have a baby one day." He smiled and seemed very proud to make this announcement.

Ned explained, "General George Washington, being a Southern gentleman and a plantation owner, was not happy about the idea of arming blacks and allowing them to fight. When he took command of the Continental Army in Cambridge near the beginning of the war, he did not want to allow free or enslaved Blacks to fight. However, after considering the offer the British made to free slaves who would fight for the Crown and his own need for fighting men, he changed his mind. He changed his orders to allow free Blacks to fight. Many slaves hoped to obtain freedom for themselves and their families by running away and joining the Continental Army by passing as free men. Other slaves were sent as substitutes for their owner or their owner's sons with the promise of freedom, if they survived." Mrs. Jessup interjected, "some slaves were freed, but for other slaves the promise was never kept." Ned continued, "Men and boys between the ages of 11 to 70 went to fight for the freedom of a country that enslaved them."

"You may think it is odd that as man of color, I would be part of this fight," said Ned. "At the campfire last night, the soldiers in my cannon regiment asked, why with so many of my people being enslaved in America, would I want to fight for the slaveholders? This seemed especially odd to them considering the British offer to set slaves free if they served the King,"

"I told them about being at the Pennsylvania State House ("Known to us as Independence Hall where the Liberty Bell is," the teacher chimed in.) when Mr. Jefferson's paper was read. In it he talked about how he thought, 'these truths to be self-evident, that all men are created equal, that they are endowed by their Creator with certain unalienable Rights (that means God gave us freedoms that no one should take from us), that among these are Life, Liberty, and the Pursuit of Happiness.'

I thought these words were grand. I thought to myself if this country becomes free, maybe someday all my people will be free. As far as why didn't I fight for the British? Just look at how they treat their own people. We are taxed without representation. There are things we cannot buy unless His Majesty's stamp is upon it! It seems to me Fat ol' King George treats all of us as if we were slaves. I don't trust him!"

"I hope the General is thinking of freeing his own slaves. I think the General was pleased and amazed that so many of us colored people are fighting and serving with courage."

"What about you Ned?" asked the children.

"I was born into freedom, thanks to my Daddy. His ability to train and handle horses was useful to him. We settled in Indian country called Conshohocken about twelve miles up from Philadelphia near the Schuylkill River."

The children nodded at the recognition of familiar names and places near their hometown.

18

Ned continued, "I had to report to Colonel Proctor's Regiment in Brandywine to defend Philadelphia from the Redcoats. We were being thrashed pretty badly. I don't know if you learned that in your books. But we suffered many heavy losses." Ned lowered his head sadly.

"Many of those men were my good friends. In some battles we barely had time to say a few prayers or even bury our soldiers. The redcoats are cruel and ruthless with the bayonet. The bayonet is a nasty weapon that causes horrible wounds. I think a whole lot of them blighters are just waiting out there somewhere to ambush us."

Some of the children jumped up to peer out the window, anticipating another unexpected arrival. Mrs. Jessup cautioned the class to simmer down and show respect for Mr. Hector.

Ned became very quiet. With hesitation, he spoke, "Forgive me young men and maidens, my courage fails me, but never the less I must ask and I must know … How did we fare in our revolution? Did we win or lose?" Ned steadied himself like as one preparing to hear bad news. The children looked at each other and sang out in chorus,

"We won! We won!"

Ned, with his gun lifted high, shouted joyously, "Huzzah! Praise Almighty God!" He took a minute to calm himself, and with almost a look of embarrassment at his show of excitement, he went on, "Forgive me!"

"You don't know how often we have been thirsty, hungry, tired, ill, filthy, ragged, freezing in the winter, roasting in the summer, and always longing to be with those we love, all the time not knowing whether we would die today or tomorrow or even the next moment and if it would be worth the sacrifice. How could a ragged army of farm and merchant boys defy the world's best-trained and equipped army? We didn't know if we could win, but we knew we had to try!"

Ned had a sudden flash of realization. "The General," he said, "what happened to The General?"

"He died," Sam said sadly.

"No!" interrupted Seth. "That's not what he's asking. The General became our first President."

Ned was perplexed. "A president? What's a President? Hope that's not just another name for a KING!" An angry fire flared in Ned's eyes. "We are fighting to get rid of one tyrant, we don't need another!" he said through clinched teeth.

"Ned, a President is not like a king," the class tried to explain.

"Tell me how that is?" urged Ned.

Suddenly distracted, Ned cocked his head as if he had just been called by an invisible voice. He ran to the window and turned to the class and said, "They're coming!"

"Remember us, remember why we fought! Remember to care for your freedom and don't misuse it! Just because you have your freedom doesn't mean you will always have it, unless you guard it well! We will fight and if need be die, for you to have it!"

Ned was now moving to where he sensed the voice. "I must get back! Maybe I'm the one that makes the difference in whether we win or lose." He paused to look at the children once more. "Maybe it is you that will make the difference whether your family, community, or even the freedom of our country continues. I must go!"

Ned ran urgently out of the classroom as quickly as he had come in. He disappeared into a smoky blue mist. The bell rang. It was dismissal time for heroes of old, and heroes to come.

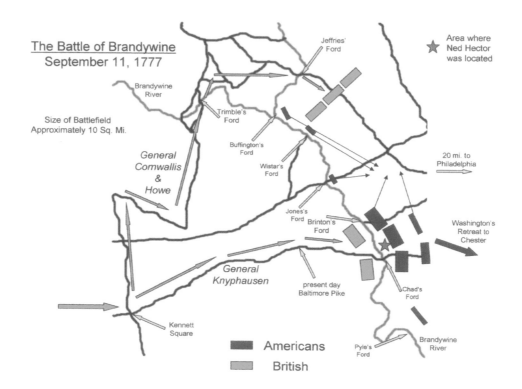

The Battle of Brandywine
September 11, 1777

Brandywine River

Size of Battlefield Approximately 10 Sq. Mi.

General Cornwallis & Howe

Jeffries' Ford

Trimble's Ford

Buffington's Ford

Wistar's Ford

Jones's Ford

Brinton's Ford

General Knyphausen

present day Baltimore Pike

Kennett Square

Area where Ned Hector was located

20 mi. to Philadelphia

Washington's Retreat to Chester

Chad's Ford

Pyle's Ford

Brandywine River

Americans

British

Map of the Battle of Brandywine

From The Mouth of the Story Teller

My name is Noah Lewis and I love to tell about the people, places, and events of the colonial times, especially of my people's history. Who are "my people"? My people are those who did willingly come or were forcibly brought to this land, and by their effort made and were made by a community called America. You might ask, if you are an American, then why do you say "my people" as if you are a separate part of the whole?

Before I was asked to come into my daughter's fifth grade classroom and give a talk on colonial America, I had no concept of black colonial history. American history, yes! I had been taught that all throughout my schooling. But all I knew of black colonial history was of Crispus Attucks. Then why was I asked to do this talk? During this time I had been working on my genealogy. I had gotten back to a relative named Noah Lewis born 1800. I also had run into a brick wall. In my desperation to find Noah Lewis's parents I started searching the pension papers of the Revolutionary War in hopes of finding something. I found nothing. But in the search I came across a book written by Charles Blockston named Black Genealogy. In it I learned of a man named Edward "Ned" Hector.

Something I have noticed as I have taken part in many Revolutionary War re-enactments, there are very few blacks who attend them. Perhaps many blacks, unaware of our history, felt the way I did; that is, "Why should I be interested in learning about a bunch of poor slaves?"

Edward Hector was so very different than what I thought about black colonials. First, he was a free man. He was one of many free blacks that lived during this time. Secondly, he was a soldier. He was listed on the muster rolls as a bombardier with an artillery company. Thirdly, he was a teamster. Teamsters or wagon drivers were well paid, specially trained and highly skilled people. Fourthly, he was independent thinking and courageous. Fifthly, he was considered and respected as being heroic. Finally, he was so well regarded in his community that he had a street named after him in 1850. He was one of very few blacks I know of that had anything named after them in the mid-1800s.

What has been wonderful about my educational journey is that as I learn of one notable black colonial, I am led to another. What a rich and amazing history we have! The originator of our national seal included a motto with it, "e pluribus unum," the many that become one. My goal is to tell the black part of the "pluribus," who was part of the many that enabled this nation to be free.

I don't want you thinking of Ned as a story, but as someone who was real, someone who represents another facet of the colonial African-American experience. It is my hope for all to find pride in our black colonial history. I hope Americans, who are not of African ancestry, will realize they owe part of their freedom to and be grateful for these amazing people. I hope we Americans, of African ancestry, will take a greater pride in our colonial ancestors, both enslaved and free. We all need to celebrate them all!

Figure 4. *Two Teamsters of the Continental Army's Corps of Waggoners, 1779.*
One has a brown coat, green jacket, buckskin breeches, white yarn stockings, and felt hat. The other wears a nankeen coat, brown jacket, green breeches, blue ribbed stockings, old shoes, and beaver hat with a white button.
Source: From *Pennsylvania Packet*, 20 March 1779. Drawing by author.

109

Civilian Dress

Hat - The hat came in many styles, not just the tri-corner type. It depended on the need. It could a stocking type if you were poor or gold threaded if you were well off. I wear a broad brim as a teamster because I need the shade and protection from the rain and sun. [See "cockade" to find out why one side is up.]

Civilian Coat - Remember I spend most my life outside. This coat serves as protection from the elements and sometimes waste that is thrown out of the windows. It's usually long and split in the back so I can sit in chairs and on horseback. The buttons on my sleeves were put there to discourage me from wiping my mouth and nose on my sleeves.

Neck Stock - I wear a triangular piece of cloth much like the Boy Scout's neck wear. I can use it for many purposes, such as a neck warmer, bandage, sweat band, tourniquet, napkin, or a sling. When it becomes thread bear I can cut it up for patches for the gun or sell it to the cloth monger who will turn it into paper.

Cockade - This decoration on the hat held one side of the hat up. This also could communicate what side one's loyalties belonged. By holding up one side of the hat, it would allow me to carry something long like a gun on my shoulder. Normally it was the left side that was cocked up.

Waistcoat - This piece of clothing allows me to keep my body warm and allows me to remove my coat without out me being in the public in my underwear. [See blouse.] I might leave the third or fourth button from the bottom undone as a manner of being stylish. If I take my coat off you will notice the back of my waist coat is split. This will allow for my ever growing prosperity to be evident around my midsection [that is to say my fatness] without needing to buy a new waistcoat.

Blouse - This pull over shirt, with a collar and v-neck opening, is really my under wear. [Yes, it's my only underwear since you wondered.] At night I remove all clothing accept the blouse, which is actually is bundled in my breeches during the day and goes down to my knees when everything else is taken off. I wear it just about all the time. It can be made of cotton, or linen.

Breeches - Breeches were a sign of manhood. A young boy would spend much of his childhood in a dress like his sister. This way it was easier to potty train children, who were outside most the time anyway. When a boy became old enough for his mother to make him breeches, they would have a breeching ceremony. This celebrated the boy becoming old enough to go out with his father and do a full days work. [about 12 to 14 hours]

Stockings - These are very long socks that go above the knee, they keep my lower leg warm and protected. These are much easier to replace than pants with shredded legs.

Garters - These are small belts, tapes [ribbon], or ropes that when tied around the top of the calf, would hold up one's stockings.

Belt - My belt is used more to hold my tools [knife, tomahawk, whip, purse (Yes, I said purse! We men carry our money in a purse. It's the style.), etc.]

Half Gaiters - These are ankle and shoe coverings are worn to keep sticks, stones, and objects out of my shoes when I'm in the woods. These are also called spatter guards from which the term "spats" comes from. [Ask your grand parents.]

Shoes - In general shoes were not made right and left. They are made the same. They were made right and left by wearing them. When they wore down on one side of the shoe, you put them on the opposite foot to wear them down the other way. Most were fastened with buckles.

Tools

Gun - I can carry a Pennsylvania Long Rifle or a "Brown Bess" musket. The differences between the two guns are distance and accuracy. The long rifle is accurate from 200 to 300 yards. It's accurate because of the groves in the barrel spins the bullet. Its primary use is a hunting gun. The musket has a smooth pipe-like barrel. It starts to become effective around 80 to 100 yards. This and its poor accuracy is why the armies had to stand so close to battle. There's a hole in my gun's stock in which I can put grease to help the bullet slide down the barrel. If you look close you'll see a stone in the "hammer" part of the gun. It provides the spark to set off the gunpowder. When I am not a soldier, I use my rifle to hunt with. It is how I feed my family, since I live in the woods.

Knife - My knife is made from an old file that had lost its raspy nature. Why should I discard such a fine hard piece of metal? I can sharpen the edges and make it into a knife. It so happens that I also have the bottom part of a cow's leg bone. It died a couple years ago. Because the bone is hollow and fits my hand quite comfortably, I used it as a handle for my knife with a little cloth to cover the rough places. This is one of the most useful tools I carry. For instance, if I am out hunting to feed my family and I get a deer. Instead of carrying that heavy deer on my back for miles and miles, I can use the knife to remove the skin and meat. I wrap the meat in the skin to make it easier to carry.

Tomahawk – This tool is most useful in the woods where I spend most of my time. This axe serves me as a hammer to fix my wagon, or as something to cut wood with, or to repair my log cabin.

Tin Canteen – Sometime drinking water is not available, but I must confess water carried in tin takes on quite an unpleasant taste. I'm looking for a bottle encased in a leather pouch to hold my water. (Many objects that used lead to hold it together, like cups and canteens, also exposed its user unknowingly to lead poisoning. What you don't know can hurt you!)

Purse – This bag on my belt holds my coins (hard currency) and valuables. Of course the continental paper money they pay me with is simply worthless.

Haversack - Is a bag I carry slung over my shoulder. I carry what I need in it to survive in the woods or away from home. It's like a large pocket. Most of my clothing does not have pockets. The following are some of the things I carry in it.

> ***Tin Plate*** - I've must eat off of something.

> ***Tin Cup*** - Tin is a cheap and strong metal. I need something to drink from.

> ***Hardtack*** - This is dry hard bread. It stays edible for a long time. It's better than starving. [But not much]

Tow - This is fibers that comes from the flax plant. My wife uses it to make thread, then cloth, and then clothes. I use it in making fire. (I need a good fire to keep warm or to cook that deer meat with.)

Flint - This is a stone I use to start a fire with. When I strike it with iron I get sparks. Coupled with tow and char-cloth, making a fire is easier than rubbing sticks together.

Char Cloth - This is partly burned cloth that is easily re-ignited with a spark from flint.

Wrought Iron Fork - Good strong twisted metal that will not break on me and can resist high cooking heat.

God's Pins - Long thorns I use as straight pins to hold clothing in place. If you are well off you can afford metal pins.

Broadside of the Declaration of Independence - A big printed sheet that is posted in public places to inform the community about things.

Knapsack - Things like clothing and such, which I don't need to readily get to, I carry in here on my back.

Quill / Pen – I used a "pen knife" to cut the end of a feather to make a pen to write with.

How a cannon crew operates

Edward Hector is listed in the "Pennsylvania Archive" book as a bombardier. A bombardier is a soldier with the artillery that is capable of operating in the rear positions of the cannon. A cannon could be manned by as many as 15 soldiers and as few as 3. Five to seven could operate the cannon, the rest would defend it. The positions would vary from army to army, but in general would be like the following:

The five uniformed soldiers (for identification purposes, 1 to 5 going from left to right) had the following functions when the cannon was fired: (Not seen here is an officer who would issue the commands and the powder box.)

- #5 - the powder monkey - would run to a spot about 30 yards behind the cannon where the bags filled with gun powder would be. (Why 30 yards? Would you want to be next to this gunpowder when a lucky enemy shot struck and ignited it?) He would grab a charge (bag) and carry it to #4.
- #4 would receive it behind his back, and then put the charge in the cannon's barrel.
- #1 would ram (push) it completely down the barrel.
- By now #5 would have given a cannonball to #4 who would place it in the barrel.
- #1 would ram it snuggly against the gunpowder.

- #2 would use a long thin spike to push in to the touch hole at the top and rear of the cannon to puncture the gunpowder bag inside.
- #2 then would prime (fill the hole with gunpowder) the touch hole
- #3, who has been holding a slowly burning piece of rope on the end of a pole, upon hearing the command to fire would touch the glowing end of the rope to the gunpowder and the cannon would fire.
- #4 take the other end of the ram, which would have spiral shaped fingers on it called a wormer (he's presently holding one), insert it in the barrel to make sure the barrel is clear of any obstructions,
- #1 then dips the swab or sponge into water and pushes it into the cannon to put out any burning embers that still may be in the barrel. (Who wants to put gunpowder into a barrel with red hot embers? Not I!)
- #2 has his thumb over the touch hole. When the sponge is removed a pop is caused by the vacuum created by not allowing air in through the touch hole. The heat of the barrel evaporates the water or sometime a swab (a piece of dry cloth or wool on a stick) is used to dry it.
- Now we're ready for another volley (shot).

Did you notice the man and woman dressed in civilian (non-military) clothing? The man, like Ned, could be a teamster or wagoneer (wagon driver). Ned, being a soldier (bombardier), could step into position #2, #3, or man the powder box if they were killed or wounded. The woman would be like Molly Pitcher, bringing water to the cannon. There were a couple Molly Pitchers. The one of The Battle of Monmouth fame was married to Private Hayes, one of Ned's fellow Artillerymen with Proctor Third Pennsylvania Artillery. Her name was Mary Hayes. "Molly" is a nickname for Mary. Notice the water is for the "cannon" and not the men. Now you know why!)

Historical Fact & Fiction

The following is a special note to the adults that will be sharing this story with kids. I have occasionally read historically based, fictionalized books. As much as I enjoyed the stories, many left me confused as to what was true and what was not. I don't want my readers to be confused. Let your young readers know that the subjects about Ned and his times are true. Only the time travel and modern day plot line are fictionalized. There is some information that although possibly true, is inferred for the sake of enhancing the reader's understanding. For example, I talk about Ned hearing the reading of the Declaration of Independence. I don't know if he was really there in fact, only that he could have been. I don't know what his plans were to have children, only that he had a son. I assume he learned how to handle horses from his father, although there are other ways he could have learned. The "orders" are made of composite facts to introduce Ned. I am speculating as to the reasons why Ned was working for the military. The information about what happened in the Battle of Brandywine and where Ned and His regiment were located is true. In the back of this book are the facts about Edward Hector. I put them in to clarify what we do know. Thank you.

Facts about Edward "Ned" Hector

Born about 1744 / Died 1834 at age 90

A free black man

Served as a Teamster and Artilleryman.

Fought at Brandywine and Germantown at the age of 33.

He was noted for his courage when during the retreat from Brandywine he refused to let his team, wagon, gun powder, and dropped armaments fall into enemy hands.

He was quoted as saying, "The enemy shall not have my team. I will save the horses or perish myself."

After applying three times to Congress for his pension, he received a token payment of 40 dollars the year before he died.

He lived in a cabin in Conshohocken and was buried in the area. His wife, Jude, died on the way home from the burial.

Hector Street in Conshohocken, PA was named after him in 1850.

Charles, Ned's son, would marry Leah Hector. She would live to be 106 years old. At the age of 100 she would still be chopping wood, sewing quilts, and fussing at the young girls of her time for chasing after immature boys for husbands. She would die in 1887 in the poor house after a man entrusted to sell her property ran off with the money.

About The Author

Noah Lewis is a widowed father of four living in the Philadelphia, Pennsylvania area. He has been going to schools, historical events, and historical sites presenting Black colonial history since 1996. This book is based on his in-class presentations.

Special Thanks to Fred and Alice Jewell, Thea Clark, Robert Kolva, and the re-enactment community.

For information on the **Ned Hector Programs**

presented by Noah Lewis contact Noah at **610-352-4372** or

NedHector@aol.com

For additional historical information go to **www.nedhector.com**

Printed in the United States
151144LV00002B